To Ann, who can out-hug a Bumbletum
~ S S

For the kids — Fluff, Kangaroo and the
Mole Brothers et al ~ T W

LITTLE TIGER PRESS
An imprint of Magi Publications
1 The Coda Centre, 189 Munster Road, London SW6 6AW
www.littletigerpress.com

First published in Great Britain 2006

A CIP catalogue record for this book is available
from the British Library

Printed in Singapore by Tien Wah Press Pte.

2 4 6 8 10 9 7 5 3 1

Bumbletum

Steve Smallman

Illustrated by Tim Warnes

LITTLE TIGER PRESS
London

There was a new toy
in the bedroom. He was
small, soft and floppy
and had a squidgy tummy
covered in stripes.
His name was Bumbletum.

"Hello," said Milly Mouse.
"What sort of toy are you?"
Bumbletum thought very
hard then said, "This sort."

"And what can you do?"
asked Edgar the teddy bear.
Bumbletum thought even
harder. "Something good,"
he said, "but I don't know
what it is yet."
"We'll help you
to find out!" said
the toys.

Bumbletum tried and Milly
helped, but nothing happened.

"You look a bit like a teddy bear," said Edgar. "Can you make a growly noise when you bend over like this?" GROWL! GROWL!

GROWL! GROWL!

Bumbletum tried and
Edgar helped, but
nothing happened.

"Your tail is a bit like mine," said Pip the puppy. "Can you wag it like this?" WIGGLE WAGGLE! WIGGLE WAGGLE!

Bumbletum tried
but instead of
wiggling and
waggling he just
wibbled and
wobbled . . .

and fell over.

Then another toy came over. It was Tilly Tinkler, the baby doll. "Can you wet yourself like this?" she asked, and TINKLE TINKLE! she made a little puddle.

TINKLE TINKLE!

Bumbletum was very impressed.
He tried and tried and tried, but
nothing happened.

Bumbletum was worn out. He flopped
down on the floor and had a little think.
  "I must be a 'doesn't really do anything'
sort of toy," he said quietly.
  But the other toys were sure there
was something Bumbletum could do.

"LOOK, BUMBLETUM! I'M FLYING!" Milly squeaked, but then . . .

. . . BOING! THUMP! SQUEAK! Milly fell off the bed and landed in a heap on the carpet.

"DON'T WORRY, MILLY,
I'M COMING!" Bumbletum
called as he slid down
the duvet to land flump
on the floor.

But Bumbletum wasn't ready. The bed
was very high and the floor was a very
long way down. His knees started to shake
and his tummy felt all wibbly.

"I'M NOT A BEE!" he cried, "AND I DON'T
THINK I'M SUPPOSED TO FLY!"

Boomer decided to help.
"Try bouncing a bit first, like this!" he said.
BOING! BOING!
Then Milly joined in. They bounced up and down, up and down, getting higher and higher.

BOING!

BOING!

He scooped Milly up in his arms and gave her a BIG cuddle.

Bumbletum's tummy was so soft and snuggly that Milly felt better almost at once, but she stayed a bit longer just to be sure.

"Thank you, Bumbletum," she sighed. "That's the best cuddle I've ever had!"

"CUDDLING!" Bumbletum cried. "THAT'S WHAT I CAN DO! Who wants a cuddle?"

"I know!" cried Boomer the kangaroo, bounding over. "It's your tummy!" he said excitedly.

"My tummy?" said Bumbletum.

"It's stripy like a bumblebee, and what can bumblebees do?"

"Buzz?" asked Bumbletum.

"FLY!" said Boomer, and the others all agreed.

Milly and Boomer helped
Bumbletum up on to the bed.
"Now, when you're ready,
JUMP!" the toys all shouted.

The toys all hurried over and settled down in a cosy heap with Bumbletum right in the middle. And he knew that being a Bumbletum was something very, very special indeed!

WIGGLE WAGGLE!